Betsy Fagin

Fires Seen From Space

Winter Editions, 2024

All so sun (Book 1)   7

Beauty is established   31

Movement theory   53

We have everything we need   73

Resistance is beautiful   89

All so sun (Book 2)   105

Notes & Acknowledgments   123

* * * * * * * * * * *

*All so sun
(Book 1)*

* * * * * * * * * * *

Chapter 1

Did they remember
how one spectacle
took on so much lasting?
In memory forever as
a satisfied certainty?
An increase in discomfort

is what flattened the earth.
Algorithms outmatched
previously known comforts.
Certainty cares nothing
for you or your playlists.
Suspicion holds stories together.

When people mistrust,
they depart toward cruelty,
rich with unhappiness: hard,
bitter. Believe me, I know.
I was his tennis friend
during the travel years

when Europe corresponded
with as sure a love as any
met only with *not a chance*
and *never*. Hopeful hearts
risen, soaring become
calcified into brittle authority.

Settled in nicely to a life
between exploitation
and careless possession
of the woods to walk in—
hell hardened everything
there is left to know.

Chapter 2

Crowded evenings
watch rot of matter—
no sleep, just loud talk

deeper into the head,
fundamentally asleep
there, to life.

Read the room.
Paris being Paris,
asking to see your papers.

Cops one night
while all alone—
you see what happens.

Life in another place,
beyond policing. Here
can't get away from

how this country exists
as time half-lived. Taking
advantage of living walls

around bins, metal bars,
loopholes to make
it seem like ethics exist

in business, graceful exits.
Worn down marble stairs
stay stubborn, insistent like

Black princesses,
beautiful with love
full of *No; you.*

Think about that,
we could have
what we want.

Living fast as
moving pictures like
countries with money—

plenty for expenses,
cheer yet to come.
A complete set

of sound needs would
be as safe as scenery.
Land only as background

to a romantic comedy
not just perfectly decorative
but integral, the whole point.

Plot read as sinister—
a land under occupation,
can that sound innocent?

Dollars won, cards held
invisible connections
bridge higher stakes.

What is a divine
love that's not subject
to discovery or conquest?

Impossible to map
and see beyond
limited horizons—

nothing simple, just
changed. Never quite
the same after that winter.

Chapter 3

Got closed long ago,
stood against them
on this very street.

You're going to lose
the outside to the in,
do you understand me?

This could save you:
a sealed envelope,
a coat on a hanger.

Aromantically possessed,
bodies dancing close,
hot for nothing. Just feeling

safety in music
sober restraint,
priceless, racing

curves around
expectation, eager
of some promised land.

Holding tight to the wall,
the bar, the edge
of the seat. In the arms

of dancing itself.
The floor praised,
musicians honored, breathing

together, our hearts one
drum going up the country.
Don't be followed

or cross from knowing
into watered dance floor—
sweat drinks us in, offerings

until all music stops.
Eyes lifted, mouth full
of tastes and worse,

composure. Suppose
they knew the depths
of this anger, serving only

yes, yes, I see what you mean.
You've got a good point,
absolutely. I hear you.

You're right. I had no idea,
I'm sorry. You're absolutely right.
Me? No. I'm fine. Just fine.

All the way past police
where crowds gather,
stopping street traffic to feel

the wind as living breath,
cooling the hot night,
still wet from dancing near

a table of men in a room full
of white people gathered
to redefine what a mirror is—

surface reflection only. I declare
I am determined to see everything
everywhere, in everyone.

Chapter 4

Money makes them so still,
frozen river of social graces
caricatured as boredom.

Perhaps civilization is calamity
agreed on though not discussed.
Wars waged against matter

itself, sick now with shame.
Poisoned touch, unable to smell
or taste, dull in forgotten connections—

a long time since vaguely sentimental,
detesting the good american.
Difference doesn't make an other

doesn't sicken, abandon
or shame. Now everybody's sick.
Everyone needs care.

Shops and offices call for back to work,
safe in schools and sure you can drink
the water, but have locked the doors

of the opera, shuttered theaters only
talking about the economy. Trade sullen
and lifeless for consumables.

Lost sight of evening at crowd's
edge watching darkness
disintegrate back into light.

Chapter 5

Night, but in the daytime—
hell is awfully easy to
step in, it's everywhere,
the whole street crying like this,
I sink the glass-half-full crowd,
pour one out to empty

under this arc-light
toward justice hoping
there's a back porch
to go make out on
shivering *yes* and *let's go*
mourning the bois

meeting for breakfast.
How it used to be to walk
the street with no fear
why now → why not.
Like tomorrow never happens—
I can't tell one day from the next,

her hand on me everywhere.
Sipped on slow say
with Biarritz to go to
wondering at this not quite
doubt. Not quite.
Linked through chained

thought our bondage
deserves us. Half-past
time to be asleep,
I should have known
the whole world as
a species of me's

with names and dressing
up in our put-on voices.
Recognizing thoughts
from outside as our selves.
Lying in bed to cry
in waves, then smooth

after the swell. Illumined
speech bound silent
motion into a statue
of release, zonda, ponte.
What became of wonder?
A form of wounding and rotten—

a poorly maintained well
full of grievance and regret.
Smell that. It smells better
than it tastes. You don't
want to drink it, trust me
or find out for yourself.

Spoils of the practical shaped
into a furnished room: a bed
for sleep and a mirror to look
at the self while undressing.
Noisy night markets and
open windows, lamps lit

as statements, sentences
prevailing against dark times.
The balance of letters
formed into wishes for care.
Thinking of you, thank you,
and *get well soon* written

on cards from the drawer
in the nightstand under
the window near the fireplace.
Chestnut trees and outside
tables now deserted
along the boulevard.

Nothing will ever command her
home. Too much someone's
daughter, granddaughter
cooking something frightful,
pushed up on all those years.
Too felt, too much.

Around the park, pools
form peaks, strangers sit
sentinel-like we are
on the good earth together
while injuries of certainty
like sharp angles, stick

all the way in, plumbing
the depths of difference.
What eyes see, how time
keeps. All eyes looking
for fault or for always, forever.
That isn't all you see, is it?

Would world the eyes
we have in each other,
reflecting. They eyes own her
out of what she really saw,
wonder made from looking
into or looking back.

Reflection only as far away
as the corner of lips
pressed tight. Dark streets
lit by flares light her way
along cobbles and asphalt,
back to center, back to the square.

Chapter 6

Left off wanting forgotten thoughts—
the best friend I really have,
is knowing I-things are nasty

on the tongue.
So insulting, a mockery.
As if hell sat down

for lunch with little plates,
anger stoked tiny pitchforks—
insult to injury, telling me

you this and *you that*
and me having to give I-answers
in response, describing

qualities of sunshine
or the movement of voice
through body as sound, speaking

holy names. Meeting every why
with certainty leaves you out
here looking brand new.

Waiting on lunch—
chewed food, digestion happening
on its own, nutrients processed,

energy restored like a life
in the country with plenty,
time and agency.

No news, no answers
only responses to questions
rather than speeches, spectacles,

systems' mouthpiece,
thinkpiece corresponding to
smoke: nothing to grasp hold of

like hell money cinders
in morning coffee. Damp sidewalk
unhands the way forward

platforming avoidance, busy
arranging "important" things.
Prioritizing the path to market

as flower-women their cigarettes.
A smoke with coffee then
the daily papers and a hot feeling

of love that comes true in middle age,
sweat pleasantly blooming
as morning dew, a new day's dawn.

Chapter 7

Perhaps now isn't the time-window.
Why here? Why so white?
Everything looks too true.
Figured it's the end of me

if never wonder, no simplicity.
Impossible. Because god is good,
his t-shirt says so, mystic
visions recollected me to what

real reason is: material for looking,
like help must form protest or sanctions.
Intervention without me.
Our sacrifices at the shore,

in the headlands when the river
was young, remember us—we're living
this together. Living proof. So busy,
so decidedly leaving raised swords

to rust, to perish in platonic
misunderstandings. Pay the fare
for the whole world, destructions
turned into money.

Spinning golden star buried treasure
right here. Re-up feelings
of generosity if you have them.
Who are your people?

Are they generous? Kind?
In marble-topped time capsules
from before the triumph
of manners—what it is to be

cheerfully alone—was rotten
through with shame. Wasted
luck. Should've celebrated
when we had the chance.

Nothing now is inconsequential.
Living matter crossed into dance,
a joyful imitation of never waiting
and money enough for lunch.

Rabid wanting smiles and waves.
Movement of stones shaped
into terraces perchance seating
there, for beaten love loves to win.

Internally trained to cheerfulness,
externally stood in crowds, silent.
Salient qualities detached from reason
as surely as this *Now* adventure unfolds—

longings gone, spring returned
with a healthy conceit and nervous
tension. Soreness, traffic, some moron
or other. I misjudged myself rather than you.

Chapter 8

Telling this street from that.
Crossing what's deeply thought
with confidence, place, relevance,
authority. What makes him
so sure? Maybe he's disinformed.

All he knows are written things: *bad*
and *not that bad*. *Trouble* and
dinner. Invite him to imagine *we*
or weather, *whether not* what
we share—this air, water, all so sun.

Remembering relational as being
alone, outside, with a sad past.
I always take the river one bank at a time
back to you, your dislikes, hates
and incapacity to shift

where no wonder once was.
It cannot journey through,
stays stuck, in certainty, insulated
from flowing with the current
toward being, not just waiting.

Chapter 9

> I know I have lived enjoyment
> very much not because
> of wounds or love turned
> to business. I count revolutions,
>
>
> seen enough to know
> dusty old systems that finish
> your sentences without ever
> letting you talk. In any corner
>
>
> of the world, wellbeing for friends
> and enemies alike. Built into
> the foundations, the policies
> and procedures in place to convince
>
>
> our connections don't count.
> Matter of fact, divorce yourself—
> sit across the table from us, estranged.
> Wear a watch-chain, a monocle maybe.
>
>
> Count gold, puff on cigars while others
> serve you. Never mind cloud recognition—
> once it was ice, the same liquid
> in your own body, salted and spread
>
>
> into ashes and smoke, gas light,
> some sticks. Let that connection count,
> credit more than money costs.
> Worth more than our usefulness

and productivity. Worth more than
thousands of acres in trade—
knowing this hell of a world
held together.

Recognition quietly locked away
is why it hurts so much. Flour on
the shelves again, more to feed
the babies with than just milk powder,

and talking about times gone.
Everything remembers how
it used to be, but won't remember
forever, eventually forgets.

Chapter 10

Upstairs an opened door—
bells rang through the night,
I mean sirens. Drove me
away from tranquility, pushed
me to standing, daring

night to feel sorry for the
sleeplessness and worry,
the calls to poison control—
good looking out. Water
will help, sleep. I count

blessings, sun kissed.
Count absurdities and take
notes. Softly sung something
repeated, all of it a nightmare,
wishing it were different

than it is. What's gone? All time:
before and long ago both
dance close together, pressed
tight. This future is shrugged
shoulders, is whatever.

I don't personally future,
but support some dancing
again. Something with enjoyment,
something splendid,
something dear.

Late last night remembered something
about the day. Day always centered,
day taking up so much space.
This is a time of darkness, of inner
work. Day is all roses, water

in earthenware jugs filled
with forgiving, with liberty.
Freedoms flower in light and warmth,
fortunate with slippers, bathrobes
and nice, hot showers. Mail arriving,

family, good friends, home
and no-trouble guests received
with great pride. The word *yes*
on our lips with many *thank-yous*.
Don't stop. Music over money

to give the drummer some
soaked in brandy, antiquities.
Want-led lives playing at happy.
Beaming because they
haven't yet seen the bill.

* * * * * * * * * * *

Beauty is established

* * * * * * * * * * *

Every planet is beautiful

Even all these years later,

honor to all, favor to none.

You are beautiful.

Your planet is beautiful.

And all of it will burn—it's burning now.

Of all eleven dimensions and eighteen worlds,

this one, all but extinct, related by dualities

held together only by relationships

that appear in position, each theory

a different aspect of a single underlying theory:

Can science save us?
- The rain dance? *(not the clematis)*
- The gift of four winds? *(no one regrets trying things)*
- Project skywater? *(altering oceans, reshaping cloud cover)*
- Giant mirrors? *(20% chance of success)*
- Synthetic trees? *(making use of old oilfields and coal mines)*
- Forests of the seas? *(plankton grasslands, algae prairies)*
- Cloud shield? *(women & children cast off previous lives)*
- Ocean pumps? *(iron seeding, misreading cues)*
- Sulfur blanket? *(explode the volcanoes)*

How well do we know our neighbors?

    People trapped in situations, wanting

        radiant health, kindness,

compassion, gladness. Equanimity

    for everyone.

Suspicious of shifting

A world suspicious
of shifting where man tools
cut light and women
acted wood-stained
for decoration, nothing more.

A landscape within me
devoid of each other,
opposite abandoned
playgrounds for rain shelter
wood chips, fruit pips

mask of compliance
and invisibility cloak
seal in my own dead cells
run off after the revolution—
washed up mylar on the rock shore.

Matter theory : the cave is collapsing

nations must sacrifice
linear for adventure
to feel again

spontaneously alive
our effigy selves
resting in power

of inner sanctuaries
grown beloved
so union guised

at one with our
people and animal
surroundings in

keeping with the trees
presumptuous this desire
to control or be controlled

Every planet we reach is dead

a sane sky knows no rank
here everyone can win

circling status
peregrine

sexual blurring
haunted bounty

herds of fortune cloud
winter sister to her tired

of weighing racial mixture
part foreign soils

body foreign
allied emotion

steady fulfillment until taken ill
with trouble winds blowing

grounded drones
ghost money

Against empire

1.   Leave what we built here ———

                                      ———light not promised

    ———what a woman can feel

            slowly coming to a boil.

First consult the birds then   raise a glass

            to the end

                  of empire.

2.   What money can buy

             the experience of sound?   Not the idea of an orange

        but the taste of an orange,   sticky sweet.

            An empire of stars in denial

                sunlit barricades   flowering branches,

           fists blooming. A chance meeting is a bird,

                tired of being tired.

3.   Keep what you think you own.

4.   Ancient magics
                                 almost   lost

         sow day into night interpretation
  of bird flight's material heart.

                         Always
        take the money.

            I will bury your empire.

                         Earth, everyone my witness.

5.   Left on this paywalled

              planet we are your   oracles

     wilting on the vine

                   eventually harvest

     attention ─────

              always too expensive to buy

                   I feel safer already.

6.   All the peacemakers'

         hearts colded.

                Direct interventions follow long-winged birds through

     salt tears,   impatience,   curiosity.

Gratitude

         a simple offering

                        opens portals.

Auspex

Kestrel cannot digest
swords or make bread
of empire's machinery.
At its apex,
an imagined self,
the center—

presumptuous,
arrogant, competitive;
taking your body
and replacing the head
with my own sacred
boundary.

Water sources cut
or poisoned, I must
plunder myself—
trees sprouting in open
country, abandoned buildings
with no profit motive,

just get it done.
Results not excuses
clustered along river valleys
channeled with bridges
and walls—disease frontiers
prove borders indefensible:

auspex, intimacy, welcome
or not. Infinitely porous
and bound up in each
other with no fear
of inevitable reinvention,
improvement is possible.

Mapping a new era

Dew headed window daze
loves early morning premonitions.

I have my own flag,
currency, postage stamps

and many other unreleased projects
to attend to: not just *the rebels*, but *the flesh,*

crystal ball, madhouse. A cold planet
disguises our case for war. Floating

villages from the temple moons come
to life again: street theater challenges

behavioral change not just sensitivity
trainings with free fruit and music. Windfall

shame on "appropriate for a girl"
this golden thread to secret future

weddings like cold silk, all
our strategic alliances.

Magic theory : amorphous sexuality

"love symbol #2"
was sent to us through magic,
a missive *(I'm not
a woman, I'm not a man)*
from one of the eleven
dimensions after disbanding
the revolution:

○ free food

○ you are "mine"

○ my open yes

○ "my" bursting heart

○ galactic deeper

○ emotional force

○ twelve clouds of joy

without ever saying love—
convenient fiction,
an open clearing
in an otherwise dense
wood inflamed
the only tree left
under which to awaken.

Suspiciously fixed

All confidence masks,
invisibility cloaks,
plastic bags of indifference
slipped on in the rain-
abandoned playground.
Stained decoratively
yellow leaves,
birch not beech, shade
light-devoid landscapes.
Suspicious of myself.
No rank, no status
to haunt the soil.
Heightened desire
is a foreign body,
foreign emotions—
not from here.
Still allied, alien,
never forgetting
hunger in the midst
of plenty.

Having brought order

    We are finally crest
    point fallen. Investigation
    results received—
    arrest their leader.
    Determination masquerading
    with something to prove
    to profit, population
    the tens and tens of people
    on the internets who have

    known shelter and dinner.
    The best chocolate cake,
    a cloth handkerchief
    for hours. Menacing
    messages across Europe
    gave so much adverse
    yet remains popular
    despite what you say.
    How can he?

How on earth
can you answer that
with I thinks and I feels,
I feel and I burrow
I cave and am embarrassed
I can make no protest
I am forced. I play
despite losses and call
for winds, for rain.

Lodos

> I don't like the look of
> this particular manifestation.

> Streets full of chanted fire,
> more often heard than seen.

> We are active at night, braver
> than no questions asked.

> All stars are also patience,
> visions of the long departed.

> A sorry wind, our silent flight
> transforming the mess

> of worn down earth and stone:
> lurking in dry wells, cool hollows.

> Never coming back to that
> planet again. What they see

> now with their million eyes
> we can only dream—

> clicking noises, a rasping hiss
> beyond what we are capable of.

No longer steady state

Far away from all is well
into absorption of evidence.
I expected to see change, but
what's in seeds now is classified.

Roots mistake illusion for diminishment.
Bricked over borage, clover,
chrysanthemum, natural deterrents.
Arsenic hour promises—

the formula for success
is not three-hour meetings
or focus group dynamics.
Compass points to outcomes—

our survival imagined us
summering within the
kingdom's embrace
of riot and meltdown.

When emergency management
cut down all the trees
for their staging area, did they
mean to leave that one?

Seeded clouds

My sailing ship will be earthbound.
Cast off & left behind looking foolish,
people will gamble and people will pay.
We are not shops or supermarkets.

Seeding the clouds takes science out
of the laboratory and into the skies
for no more rainy days over theme parks.
Observing impacts, increasing atypical futures

they insert errors, have reserved
the right, will charge future fees
to decline access to services—*you belong
here with us*—engineering and art

where there used to be talking. Bejeweled
psychics in velvet caravans making
predictions on us, our index card minds
putting things in order, even by the sea.

Earth Store

    Disintegrating hopes of rescue back
    into midnight: curse up believing

    in anything. Common blue violets
    bloom all try-hard (deer-resistant)

    under the black walnut through holes
    and cut-out toes. This drastic change

    of weather is woven linen, a cornflower
    ribbon divider marking out days of belief

    in grand houses, library magnificent
    with high ceilings, textiles, ornaments

    disappeared back into market stalls.
    Nature will rise against nature, through it.

.

What seeds were planted?

Bicker backstabs: you're no flower.
Not a goddess drowned to disappear
into ice creams and movies.

You are not a mountain or a lake,
just a human being. Human enough
to use tools and maybe hike along the water

to dismantle or just collapse at seeing
the old neighborhood's crumbling.
Walls caved in that half-sleep way

like money jobs are community or pretend
family sensed from within projection, provoked
to defend and attack an utterly vulnerable self.

No barricades can save or uninvite this
opposite of welcome. Blood-kin anger
trades numbness for accountability.

Forcefields of encouragement
all but disappeared—utterly selfish
without the self-esteem to be useful.

Wounded hearts run through with regret:
it's why we hardly speak. Everything a curse:
hot oven in a heat wave.

Movement theory

Movement theory : bystanding

bystanding invisible worlds'
performance unaware
of its grand leading role

playing right by walking
sixteen dancers embraced
extending partnered arms

shadow moments where
dancing is protection
arched them all in shadow

lurking over what protects.
does it serve? does the ground
tremble under boots and sneakers

amid straw plucked
from shattered glass
direct a gaze that carries

what is an appearance
of hair and skin, gait
into a different stance

sameness cataloged
appearing white, mostly male-
presenting ballerinas looking

through layers of phones,
fists for hands, extra bags
for burdens (brought their own)

pockets full of fist
headphones for light
guiding shadowed seas

to wall the ground
and wall in change, trying
to fix a distant horizon

Going to Mars for a better view

Tasting disrespect, ground
into soil to aerate the mud
of living waters, witness
our animal owed hearts.

Squat gods, their repossessed
cathedrals and fortresses, shot through
grave land leaving only a rubbled sense
of escape: of ancestors, homelands.

Self-representing nations making up
flags and theme songs, I mean anthems.
Sequin sky mirrors a watercourse way—
plowed fields scorched, grown resistant.

Movement theory : safety

Safety nest is more closet wall
than idealistic crusade: something
to lean against, find resource—

feeding phoned in, hidden from light.
Protected from shady occasions
dressed up elegant like rivers flowing, listing

full of easy conversation and a sickening
aversion in the throat and stomach
to saying anything contentious,

anything at all about any one of us—
we don't want any trouble—
noting instead new changes in the wall

and in the ground itself: *sorry
about the mess.* Shadow partners play
their roles guided by whatever

is heard through headphones—
sameness and difference
bind the galaxy together.

Before the dark times shadow them all,
over-protectant for just a moment.
Invisible worlds standing by.

Going to Mars alone

Going to Mars will be all of us,
the fishes and fish keepers
their honorifics, the praise givers,

the shrine goers, sick and tired
tied to the ground. Tires to elevate
us up through sky heaven water

cyclone spiral up from parched earth,
praise be, shorts-wearing guards
arm the border, enforce periphery:

us and them gutted. Shirtless bystanders
ice onlookers wandering near
the quest gates for faith long gone

dropping through the dry earth.
All that's wet will be frozen,
plowed fields scorched water

away into glass. My nations
present a self-renewing whole,
taking it to the gods

demanding squat. Lion-hearted
frame upon frame,
our animal friends witness

tilling the soil, encamped
emperors fly on horseback
as every steward of the land:

plow, toil, my back a plague
of frogs, fish, locusts—sore & old
all come to the watering hole

our dead now bones, our mollusks
our starfish all that's left of us,
outdated components, our offerings.

To divine and center

Help reconstruct insistent
meaning. Mutual dreaming

binds as expanse to contract.
Unpredictably adaptable

structuring moment by moment—
from hypothetical past and imagined

Black futures: full to overflowing
with peace and ease. Swallows warned me

about the threats to my life. Severity
retrained into restrained chaos,

able to hold discomfort and compulsion
with necessary care. Reduced

to spare-change this complex
fragile kernel of acceptance.

How a body moves to music

A body moves to music
instinctively understanding

beautiful. Notes getting out
of bed helps living into questions

of how air is an interface where
relationship begins not only touch,

but conversation, dancing. Thought
is unspoken speech flowing across a room

exploring the roof of your mouth, tongue,
teeth, jaw: valid interests. Distant curiosity

at a rippling soundscape. Fountains,
cricket chorus as waxing speech. Waking

is grace, *still alive* a response. Equal actions
balance above and below, mirrored

in any movement to respond, a heart moved,
moving—one beat, one step after another.

Going to Mars in pieces

Offering our components
at the shrine, given up for
blessing outdated structures.
Left like starfish,

our bones now vapor
desiccated monuments,
crystal rock salt for teeth,
all constructs abandoned.

Our wasp world edification
a balloon at the waterhole,
all lost plagues infectious once.
Undetectable is untransmittable.

My toil plow stewardship
whored back at emperors'
fallen columns newly
signed into regulation.

Mystery theory : earth mound

An inability to truly remember
pain. Lost all ways of seeing:

dragon bones stripped
in the spirit world, death-thick air

the opposite of form is always anchored:
not emptiness, burial grounds, haunted

mansions, streets, laced fenders,
white strollers, memorial bicycles,

the hole they dug for us
with a fountain to draw us down

is this reverence? Or is it a trap?
A mirrored box filled with honey.

Mother theory : resolution

Don't you resistance me.

I will turn into an exclamation point.

Punch someone in the eye.

Trust is the only real currency.

Glued to a girl with a pearl earring

Delimiting terms of melting
glaciers created from lakes, into lakes.
Earth deep lava, explosive growth
that mounts to stars, become planets
in the same pattern of everything born—
animals, plants. Bloom, wither, die.

Peel off stuck skin, grow again—
first leaves from sprout, fragile
seedlings from seed. Closer
and closer to decay. The body forever
complicit in violence, corruption—
not good, in terms of shelf-life.

Just flesh and its ailments,
predisposed like relatives
I never heard of and *changing
the conversation* tactics forever.
Unexamined internal processes
disappear as soon as they arrive.

Mystery theory

        no one calls

no freedom tower

                the masks

                      the pile

      a pool

of remember

                leaving

                      a lover as

                          tactical

                    withdrawal

          not romantic defeat

              distraction disperses focus

        dream a planet closer than the sun

                  with water for drinking

                    the difficulties of a daylit life

        gravity overcome is an asset

      all the glass windows

               finally to myself

rain scaffolds a silvered city

                  universes

        created at will

reflective

        of this circled-wagon time

                in all the worlds

Latent root

    frozen lies still
    pray for us
    if you believe

    in planting
    synthetic trees
    carbon suck

    our drugged
    waterways
    moss wall—

    don't say
    no one noticed
    or no one tried

    blasphemy
    is only
    for believers

Going to Mars for privacy

        my world balloon wasp nest
        edification of all construction
        all abandoned monuments
        dried up oracle fumes, vapors
        disrespected like all regulation
        all traffic signs
        columns fallen relic now
        grave statuary, shot through
        fortresses, cathedrals
        picking over the last of
        ancestors' homelands
        looking for clues of escape
        making sense of rubble
        cherry-picked skulls to
        explore new lands
        carrying hidden seeds
        scaffolding tinted observation
        the whole herd of us
        not looking down, looking up

Mystery theory : excessive heat watch

Ice our gods.
Their seen-
through cracks

belie disguise
of invisible injury
and isolate.

The most ballingest
kneels at my shrine
in business

leathers drenched
in phone light,
eyes averted.

Sick from
all that cake.
Double the gates.

Love to market
rivers, listen more
than talk. I hear

our fires
are seen
from space.

* * * * * * * * * * *

We have everything we need

* * * * * * * * * * *

Desperate hours

Unbound, revolving,
most deliveries
arrive safely
tempering twilight
and dawn. Must
retrieve know-how
for this system—
memory of rebellion,
survivalist vitality.
Information access
has failed, offering
only overwhelm
not inspiration.
My fear and I attack.

Requests for my
presences still
alive against all rule.
Candles consulted
an interior universe—
I am regret, struggle,
bare teeth to the horrors
of a half-known life:
no touch, torments,
believing myself
broken, too poor
to rebuild
the you of me
as affirmation.

Eating ancient virtue

       Illustrated hands pair
       with another halting source
       then run, coursing
       seed vision the obvious
       suspicion—alone
       in the abundant multiverse—
       then part, fast enough
       brought on the unexpected.
       Cannot destroy mesa noise
       or shift dirt-done stance
       to allow lost ways to erupt
       or fall her. Fail. Disturb
       an accidental nightmare
       bone-mist of dream-surety
       open expansion the only
       constant, deception. Non-
       disclosure misdirected.
       Crucial don't stop collected
       tears manifesting my present
       existence including my trod
       on stood ground.
       Laboratories conceal nothing.
       Scorched restraint rarely
       connects our breath now
       frozen underfoot. Accept
       the unstoppably
       simple bouncing
       within false complexity.

Backwater planet

Seed threats model desire
just as twin suns
we are close to rising

juices, innate spirit
half hidden in the smoke—
destruction of old forms

while enduring the deepest
most open, radiant spaces.
Thought I'd be dead by now,

postponed not canceled.
Survivor syndrome practicing
at empowered flesh,

pretending a voice to speak in
lighthearted and brick
that window to survive and thrive.

Unguarded moments
within the five fires
some kindness for our broken

hearts. The new day
announced, even here,
rewiring suffering.

What tulips once were
(don't be afraid to act alone)

Paper ruled all of life—
a lasting peace that resources
the comportment body.

Morning risen,
to recognize coherence
in the face, internalize

protocol, convinced of it
with seeing eyes.
More than what is beautiful

summoned by fragile
demands sat down in a corner
with the rest of the timed-out city.

Excruciatingly slow
to transition to girl
or woman, fin to fly.

Rock dove from red brick
to dizzying heights
of tar beach flocking, flown

knowing much more
than what's seen with conviction—
a piece of paper can ruin lives.

Act natural

And notify supervisors.
Their information charts
and database not truth
just urgent, just vital
pairs well with basic
survival fears. Sleeping
with desperate
spreadsheets
and a need-to-know
basis. What worth
pledged as unity
when we many one
keep the memory
of systems generating
understanding
way worse than
stick rock throw
this essential service.

Civic duty

        Water to pay for what
        we already charge the sun,
        this is a serious moment
        in time. We're losing
        everything for the same
        sunrise. Leveling dawn
        as breath once complete,
        a body might have been safe.
        Understand the idea?
        Protection orders,
        sidewalk privacy.
        Streets blocked, skies
        closed, solid surface
        as impenetrable glass.
        Sheets of tolerance
        bricked like we used to
        be, like wanting to die.
        The old days saved
        our lives, for now,
        smashed, stripped our
        bad luck, suspicion response.
        Where do you get your delusions?

Whatever we want wants us

    nude diamonds
    are gold seeds

    plated with pictures
    of still making sense

    wisdom lay fallow
    like kicked-in doors

    public sky bruised
    with scarcity

    of attention
    hardship and mercy

    of caffeine and
    stimulant high for

    depths of ocean
    fulfillment, mutual

    aid acknowledgement
    of mirror worlds

    bound in each
    other's wholeness

Luminous

Secure in nothing
bolted door brave
patiently retracing
illusions, deceptions
rid of intimacy
support turned to a ghost
sent down roots
to solidify what's worthy.
Frozen breath burrowed
below granite slabs,
workers demanding their pay
in more than money—
soaking citrus in vinegar
for solution to filth.
A freedom solution led
by stomach and pussy,
heart-light mirrored.

Early harvest

>No train fare to
>command the winds
>or make oceans obey.
>Of the five poisons
>I am the most
>lethal in this whole
>new world appearing
>from the waters.

>I know the garden
>this lot will become.

>Jasmine and hyssop-
>steeped stars.
>Let it rain and rain
>forever. Moving toward
>what approaches
>without turning
>away or expecting
>an early harvest.

In what together

    Can we, concerned, meet
    halfway with this invitation to joy
    by force to reality us all

    sane times a million?
    Herd star stuff and trees here
    across the sectioned sky toward

    right with the universe.
    Child that I am, life flows
    through forced imaginings

    to challenge the rigors of injury,
    illness, lack of sleep. Manifesting
    impatience with mutual growth,

    overwhelm. No matter rained down tears,
    precarious power of mind over mind
    green for hope of special treatment

    not lost on me, chronically self-aware.
    Ferocity freed, we could be
    having coffee right now. I would

    consider than an excellent use
    of our time. New York needs us
    strong, but not in the ways we think,

    every movement scrutinized.
    Mind reflects as light,
    fooled again to dream and want.

Wherever you are

Springtails hiding in leaf folds
know pure wisdom. True
if you believe it's true, as all
organizing principles:
magnetism, nourishment.

Of the five stars, fifteen
Saturns, nine vehicles left
you had to stumble into mine.
We didn't come into this world,
we came out of it. Emerging

whole as soothing waters'
quiet care. There might be
a good way to live. Footprints
in sand hint at this promise,
stillness just beneath the noise.

Mossy stream bench is leisurely
paced—reborn into a wasted world.
Sound is sound and silence
perfectly fused, the most
elusive inmost mysteries.

Not for nothing

        I am slowed
        across earthbound.

        Carried coast
        well wicked shallow

        dream laws crowed
        hero and murderer

        liars and cheats
        infect the earth body's

        rough wheel, seeking
        an indestructible heart.

        Break from annihilation
        from everything sin

        or forever river
        and surely

        I am perfecting
        the laws of air

and water, a river
from which many

can drink—life
cannot be stopped.

* * * * * * * * * * *

Resistance is beautiful

* * * * * * * * * * *

Resistance : in the earth

>Longing for leftover time
>a full malachite life in the mountains
>near red waters down from the skies
>as lightning driven into the earth
>filling the mountain as well as valley below—
>untold riches: name-drop that.
>White-gold that with your diamonds
>and sapphires. Platinum every day with
>copper water speech in the form of seven
>metals including the knife in your back—
>that's good steel.

Resistance : labyrinth

sundried change solidified
structure from which to form
our huts and windowless
buildings, our sanctuaries
and citadels men only women
only giving way to infinitely
more fluid transformed rigid
matter into blurred, flowing silt
silks soft washed up along
shored tension released
drops from skies beneath
the thinnest sliver of a moon-
some smile all weapons locked,
thrown knives retrieved
and safely put away, caked
in cracks whole solid ground
through which to enter
progressively smaller
and smaller unmarked
doors, gateways, portals

Resistance is beautiful

This room just needs
people. People everywhere
breathing in full, out full.
Rainbreak bridges through
smashed glass alleyways

of foundling love
are crossed rivers.
From forever's fake
treasure-pots of never
lost with want spilled out

leaf-carpeted invitations
to old absinthe rooftop parties.
Hand delivered
unseen blessings
scrawled in overthink.

Resistance compromised
(for all the candy eaters)

>Calling and hanging up
>on my future in corporate
>finance to pierce fantasies

>of sugared peoples
>tranquil nights
>our pwned city divided:

>noodle shop's a nail salon
>selling necklaces of cut
>glass on gold chains.

>Dried-out ecosystems
>in small bottles yellow
>like the sun once was.

>Boarded-up high-end shops
>painted gold to distract
>would-be looters.

Resistance : given teeth in order to attack

Renounced panic
for waterlogged tenderness
aloft across campaigns.
No rosewater, no violets,
only vapors of diligence,
initiative corroded,
this waning world.

Connect our allies, align
ourselves with enchanted
darkness focused on our own
preservation like the innermost
citadel. Network forces vast,
unhinged. Agile in the honey head
to allow the most strategic

of all recorded histories. Believing
I am broken, rippling out clear
of dust and conceit, focused
as any mountain spring to the ocean.
Rised up to rebuild.
To temper twilight and dawn,
thunderbolts against all external rule.

Resistance : blocking gov't administration
(for meth & show tunes Michael)

      Exposing broken

      heart wouldst heal

            as if trembling

                    rooms full of spies

         I sent out

              last night on

        the government in us,

    armies in our hearts

           self-consistent with love and care.

                  With *welcome all*

            in the spirit of jubilee.

Inviting them in, sympathetic

        outlaw friend-kiss like

beautiful, loving blue spirits only,

              not yellow spirits. Fixed in our ideas

                vocal on our own behalf,

            remembering sacred gifts.

Resistance : gorse

Kudzu stranglehold
without permission or
forgiveness. Wild
mountain honey downs
tools, a well change,
our best feats

charged with light.
Manzanilla can't
sleepwalk the floors
for rivers. Chicory
schemes daily along
redwood highway.

Collect it? Compel
the world floating
on our backs?
Who profits the ground
wild world uplifted?
This time becomes us.

Resistance : take the streets

Worth exploring
where the tunnel
opens warm, humid
through dusty chain-link
fence to exhausted
diablo light.

Every obvious
argument is cold
memory failing,
more coping strategy—
calima—than essential
offense—ostro, zonda

all in alignment.
We are creatures
of the pali stars—
pampero—
and the earth.
Of alizé, trees,

mountains,
rivers—
every wind.
Clinging
like fire
loves wood.

Resistance : welcome, home

        Held affection so
        tightly it turned to fear
        of passageways, women
        and their secret curtains

        imagined boundaries,
        mirrored forests,
        sovereign nations
        dissolved.

        Drowned gods, mad kings
        as offerings to a spindle sky,
        to the commons, absolute
        standing will bruised.

        Centered, in depth, in length,
        in imagination, in gladness.
        Stronger, amped up
        right-doing, arnica all.

Resistance : entire of itself

I put out subway fires with my feet.
Don't let them disappear me.
I'm venomous now and no banishing spells.

Unable to stand through rains, need to move
inland, take the Long Path away from suffering
the body doubled for sex scenes, walking

through walls wrapped in wet tablecloths.
I am the precision of a knife and all unfriendly
dogs that assume personal attack.

I seek refuge in the mechanics
of bearing witness. I am part robot
and part ghost—a mix of both.

Resist : consensus trance

Rained river bank sweet
stray, be late. Stay unflooded
sweet drainage pump
sweetwater retention units
sweetness flowing
from the tap. Ok for
consumption after boiling
barriers that hold back the sea
from particleboard houses
built across flood plains.
Here to stay.
All the new homes,
single unit and duplex,
two storeys blowing in strong
wind, on stilts. Coming
and going here, sweet rain
stay the coast that used
to be miles away. Now it's
about to eat the parish church—
the church into the sea,
the sea upon the sand,
toes, bucket, spade, legs
arms, hand it all over as
the sea hands me a whale
washed up that wouldn't
follow the mackerel trail.

Resistance : call every wind

Caught living large
in wild abandon—
CEOs' banquet
halls eating subsidies,
drunk on income smoothing,

hiding facts with rumor
and obscene milk thistle
forest floor, unceded.
No hunger stones
in the motor city bar,

doors now closed
for good. Not in any
community garden
swallowed in plastics.
Mark this time

with softness for the me
of me, love worlds
separated out sirocco
from solano, sundowner
sent to begin again.

Resistance : futile

Forgotten endurance traps
love in songbook country
harmonies wondering
about the fast lane,
big city life flat out.
Blind from sunlight
and scissor play among
ancient cut forests
and melted down paradise—
so fine, so true. Devastation
rebirths sky, refined cement
into motion toward the business
end of love—re-tasting
every shadow worlds' poison.

* * * * * * * * * * *

*All so sun
(Book 2)*

* * * * * * * * * * *

Chapter 11

Raised traffic against police
directing from the corner
and stationed at every platform
to get us all home safe.
Eight uncommon hours passed—
so much for law and order.
The street settled itself,
tears dried, screaming fell
silent, swaddled, held close
in a dance of disappointment.
Sweet willingness to surrender
to grass and trees edging
that parking lot's dubious
designation as "park."
Touched glass imprinted
with our personalities filled
with them then poured
out blessings as the world
slow-roasts, no quick fix.

Chapter 12

The outside heat could have us
all shook up the same way
some people feel damned in general.

Interpret anxiety about nothing
as anxiety about death.
Separation from anything, loss.

All possibilities never known.
After the first sip of kindness
why not have another?

Touch glasses together from hotel bar
high stools, call for cars and travel
where you can let your true face out.

Usually held close only for crying,
arms wrap around feeling ruined
wiped out, manipulated, set up.

Wanting so badly to leave,
go away ragged down
some long, dark corridor.

Chapter 13

Order the ground around
for pleasure, demand
what it gives freely anyway.

Was I myself? Wanting
winters' cold with darkness.
Yes, winter! I command it.

Requests still open,
sullen-faced, walking to work.
The sunny side shuttered

against the heat.
Awnings down.
Gate of the sun-up's

unfinished palace
and empty gardens.
Outside can be anywhere

and everywhere all at once.
The end of the line is especially
sun-hardened country: pines

and rocks up the whole
night watch, looking
for movement, signs of love.

Chapter 14

Sticks dipped in red paint
arrange an abstract heart
fixed over doorways
meaning to inspire.

Pieces of your heart are all
over town. Even in bitterness
and trouble, sweet spreads open,
fastened down into folded

fingers like prayer where
the hand is an envelope:
missive life to soak up
warmth and read about the sun

from an old easychair
near the shore. The hand
a head out of water, salt lips
right alongside beach bathers

or fishermen. The sun is afraid
of no one. No sea too open,
no harbor too close. Not even
the trash-lined, burning promenade.

Chapter 15

Never sank, never swam
just tired, floating along.
Waves break my face to swells.

Lift is whatever is buoyant in me.
Feels like sky formed me
into floating this breeze.

I paid for supper with close attention,
my currency of choice.
In that world, the only one there is,

world country rich and race
following the road ever-followed:
earth smoke, dust shadow.

Nothing abandoned touch
so tight. Arranged paper
and coin money. The sun

didn't take people so very
seriously, browned or burned,
poisoned, cancered all

like being let in
on a private joke, a punchline
always with me, never far.

Chapter 16

Left whatever normal is:
a train morning, necessary
precautions. Tipping more
than I should, no one paid
a living wage. Too many

bodies to be able to identify.
Good friends. Slow train
chemical spills and lost
passports long for a simple
life without borders.

No cascading events.
Give me a second,
I'm struggling. Add comedy
to customs. Tickets bought
on credit, climbed gates,

forty-eight minutes of tunnels—
it's fair to feel bitter.
Someone else got
what you were denied,
they didn't even earn it.

No standing in line,
no heavy bags, no constant
surveillance, no supervisors
coming in hot. Got that good
quality of life with trees

and flower boxes, ornate
architecture. Bone dry streets,
shady and cool, luxury hotels.
And then you know
what happened? Nothing.

The nothingness
is the point. How is greed
all that's happening now,
siphoned into separation—
isolates remaindered

the soil in which I grew
into a room with a balcony
that opens onto overload.
Seeing what you can't see.
Beyond rooftops to mountains.

Just staging. We still have to eat.
Apex predators are not accustomed
to resistance. Tigers stalk,
ambush, overwhelm. Maybe we
never recover, never heal.

Chapter 17

Would sincerity shield?
A table in an earthquake,
a doorframe strong back

stills ringing in the ears.
Crochetwork nailed
to walls creating a web

or tent of protection
against what mysteries
try to push through.

Netting a boundary,
cocooned but permeable.
Protected like lunch money,

kept safe, within reason.
Obscuring all complicated feelings,
everything convoluted. I overtipped

again, smelling of hair-oil,
generous like the Pyrenees with flowers.
Too much, like that second coffee.

Chapter 18

How much do we owe?
The price to the driver
had been fixed
at a hundred and fifty
accounting for gas
and congestion pricing.

Transportation strikes,
shit-covered streets
and subway platforms
makes this privilege,
this convenience worth
even more: *drive me*

to the hotel. I will pay in dust.
Connected to the land
and the beliefs of the party,
dust-powered economy.
Dust is strength, is favor.
Dust shows worth, rank, status.

Dust piles up as bought merit
and grace, beneficence from
unswept corners, under sofas
and at the edges of rugs. Sleeping
in the same room with the same
one person for the rest of your life

sounds strange to me.
Incomprehensible. I rinsed clean
of that, washed it away years ago
the way one washes a shirt,
has a cup of coffee and reads the paper
of a morning. That was before

you were born, before all this.
Back when pay phones
and telephone books. Before star
sixty-nine even. Before I found all
that wadded up cash on the steps
of Sacré Coeur. Seems strange

and suburban now, like we'd gone
to Paris only to contract Paris
Syndrome. Sick with it:
dizziness, sweating and feelings
of persecution. Having to catch
the next flight home.

Some city of lights this is.
Nothing lives up to imaginings.
Feelings of persecution follow me.
Has this programming always
been humming quietly from corners,
in the background?

Where's my hotel room,
a book to read, the free concerts,
the river, cafés where we can sit
and just listen. Take the long way
around money worry. Instead
I'm up all night fretting,

*how could we possibly,
what if* and *if only.
Who will pay? How?*
Hands shaking, road watching.
No constant swell to sail on,
just head to head, hand to mouth

ever-vigilant, seeing another
train pull out of the station.
Windows blurring, everything
smeared together, light
and shadow so quickly,
eyes unable to keep up.

Dusty, dry, needing water,
needing rest. No moving forward,
no moving back. *Penetrate
this moment to its core,
reshape it into something useful.
Wait for help or a new way out.*

Chapter 19

Never getting anywhere
through discussion:
no compromise, no humility.
Exhausted, let's coast.

Drive down along where roads
used to be before they brought in
pile drivers. Before the canal needed
to be dredged and the river dried up.

From salt marsh to Superfund—
sights: a walkway here, waterbirds,
tides were high... docks invisible
along the green road, not black.

No, the road was white, reflecting
light back toward the sky. The road
was solar-paneled storing up the sun.
The headlands, red-roofed villas,

patches of clay among the sand
forest. Ocean still blue there,
water curling along the beach's
nesting plover. Backcoast country

from sea to mountain maps how far
we'd come, from road to grass. Driver
to wanderer, through meadow
finally stumbling back into the sea.

Chapter 20

This yours? This stone-faced
sorrow hurtling toward change,
relentless and suppressed
just enough to get messy

under increased cognitive load.
Verify enormity checking balances,
confirm addresses and account
numbers for stacks. What are you

going to do for money? None of this
should have happened. Never any
money at all, table-pounding, finger-
pointing. Flipping over tables.

Explosive beliefs pound nails
into walls—everyone convinced,
physically, bodily. Hyper-confident
of their views, secret truths

everyone else is asleep to.
Mesmerized consumers crowd
without curiosity, colicky craving
soothing rain sounds, ocean

waves, adult-sized Snoos.
Rabbits dressed in human clothes,
smashing dishes, grabbing the wheel,
trying to be something they're not.

Pretending above
their abilities unseen
in the crowd—you too
can become indistinguishable,

ungovernable due to the urgency,
constant anxiety, panic,
depression, twitching, itchy skin
oozing, peeling off. Intrigued,

I'll read the transcripts later with
falcon vision, the view from above:
calm but awake to what we are
no longer: adrift.

Found our mountain,
open country where the edge
of the land meets the sea.
Wherever we feel safe enough,

where no hunger, no thirst.
This moment of freedom
strung together with others,
knots on a string telling stories,

remember how plaits mark a way,
show where opposition lurks, how
to overcome it. A route to river
mapped out, seeds for future harvest.

Notes & Acknowledgments

"Against empire" grew from a collaborative performance project *But for what's my axis?* with poets Marine Cornuet and Laura Henriksen, composer Fatrin Krajka, and artist Kara Rooney. The cross-genre performance took place at Totah Gallery in New York City in 2017.

Many of the *Going to Mars* and *Movement theory* poems were written in response to work from artists Elizabeth Bick and Dustin Yellin in the ArtFare exhibition in New York City in 2019. *All so sun* metabolizes language from Hemingway's *The Sun Also Rises* which entered the public domain in 2022.

"Glued to a girl with a pearl earring": In 2022 Wouter Mouton with Just Stop Oil glued himself to Vermeer's *Girl with a Pearl Earring* in The Hague and was sentenced to jail time for the action. I express gratitude and admiration to all actionists bringing attention to climate catastrophe.

"Resistance : entire of itself": Should the need to escape New York City on foot arise, The Long Path starts at 175th Street station and crosses the George Washington Bridge.

Quotations italicized in the text are from a variety of sources including the artist ☿, formerly known as Prince, Tami Roman, various oracles, and my paternal grandmother, Thelma Fagin Hyman.

Some of the poems in this book have appeared in the following publications: *Beloit Poetry Journal*, *Bone Bouquet*, *The Brooklyn Rail*, *DIAGRAM*, *Black WOMEN/Radical WRITING* (Hunt and Martin eds., Kore Press, 2018), *Luigi Ten Co*, and *the science seemed so solid*. Earlier versions of some poems in *Resistance is beautiful* were published as a chapbook by THERETHEN.

Thank you to all editors, readers and collaborators for your inspiration, encouragement and support.

BETSY FAGIN is the author of *All is Not Yet Lost* (Belladonna), *Names Disguised* (Make Now Books), and a number of chapbooks including *Resistance is beautiful* (therethen) and *Belief Opportunity* (Big Game Books) among others. From 2015–2017, she was the editor of the *Poetry Project Newsletter*. Her work has received support and awards from the American Library Association, *Library Journal*, Lower Manhattan Cultural Council, the New York Foundation for the Arts, and the Provincetown Community Compact. She works as a librarian and a meditation teacher in New York City, helping people navigate complexity.

Fires Seen From Space
Copyright © Betsy Fagin, 2024

ISBN 978-1-959708-11-7
LCCN 2024944704

First Edition, 2024 —1000 copies

Winter Editions, Brooklyn, New York
wintereditions.net

we books are typeset in Heldane, a renaissance-inspired serif designed by Kris Sowersby for Klim Type Foundry, and Zirkon, a contemporary gothic designed by Tobias Rechsteiner for Grilli Type. The layout and covers are done by the editor following a series design by Andrew Bourne. This book was printed and bound in Lithuania by BALTO print.

we is grateful for the support of our subscribers, and extends special thanks to recent Supporting and Lifetime Subscribers: Anonymous, Anonymous (in memory of the Beaubiens), Yevgeniy Fiks, and Elizabeth T. Gray, Jr.

Winter Editions

Emily Simon, IN MANY WAYS

Garth Graeper, THE SKY BROKE MORE

Robert Desnos, NIGHT OF LOVELESS NIGHTS, tr. Lewis Warsh

Richard Hell, WHAT JUST HAPPENED

Marina Tëmkina & Michel Gérard, BOYS FIGHT
[co-published with Alder & Frankia]

Claire DeVoogd, VIA

Monica McClure, THE GONE THING

Ahmad Almallah, BORDER WISDOM

Hélio Oiticica, SECRET POETICS, tr. Rebecca Kosick
[co-published with Soberscove Press]

Heimrad Bäcker, DOCUMENTARY POETRY, tr. Patrick Greaney

Robert Fitterman, CREVE COEUR

Karla Kelsey, TRANSCENDENTAL FACTORY: FOR MINA LOY

Alan Gilbert, THE EVERYDAY LIFE OF DESIGN

Betsy Fagin, FIRES SEEN FROM SPACE

Michael Kasper, START ANYWHERE

POSTCARDS FROM THE SIEGE, ed. Polina Barskova
[co-published with Blavatnik Archive]

Cristina Pérez Díaz, FROM THE FOUNDING OF THE COUNTRY

Sarah Riggs, LINES